W9-BBJ-634

THE GREEN BAY PACKERS

BY

MARK STEWART

Content Consultant
Jason Aikens
Collections Curator
The Professional Football Hall of Fame

NORWOOD HOUSE PRESS

CHICAGO, ILLINOIS

Norwood House Press
P.O. Box 316598
Chicago, Illinois 60631

For information regarding Norwood House Press, please visit our website at:
www.norwoodhousepress.com or call 866-565-2900.

PHOTO CREDITS:
All photos courtesy of AP Images—AP/Wide World Photos, Inc. except the following:
David Stluka/Getty Images (cover);
Author's Collection/National Football League (7);
Author's Collection (34 left); Black Book Archives (9, 15, 23 top & 36);
Topps, Inc. (14, 20, 21 bottom, 22, 34 right, 37, 38, 40 bottom left, 41 both & 43);
Complete Sports Publishing, Inc. (21 top); TCMA, Inc. (30 & 40 top left).
Special thanks to Topps, Inc.

Editor: Mike Kennedy
Associate Editor: Brian Fitzgerald
Designer: Ron Jaffe
Project Management: Black Book Partners, LLC.
Special thanks to: Karen Radtke

LIBRARY OF CONGRESS CATALOGING-IN-PUBLICATION DATA

Stewart, Mark, 1960-
   The Green Bay Packers / by Mark Stewart ; content consultant Jason
Aikens.
      p. cm. -- (Team spirit)
   Summary: "Presents the history, accomplishments and key personalities of
the Green Bay Packers football team. Includes timelines, quotes, maps,
glossary and websites"--Provided by publisher.
   Includes bibliographical references and index.
   ISBN-13: 978-1-59953-131-1 (library edition : alk. paper)
   ISBN-10: 1-59953-131-3 (library edition : alk. paper)
   1. Green Bay Packers (Football team)--History--Juvenile literature. I.
Aikens, Jason. II. Title.
GV956.G7S74 2008
796.332'640977561--dc22
                                                        2007007498

Manufactured in the United States of America.

COVER PHOTO: The Packers celebrate a big defensive play during the 2006 season.

Table of Contents

SPORTS WORDS & VOCABULARY WORDS: In this book, you will find many words that are new to you. You may also see familiar words used in new ways. The glossary on page 46 gives the meanings of football words, as well as "everyday" words that have special football meanings. These words appear in **bold type** throughout the book. The glossary on page 47 gives the meanings of vocabulary words that are not related to football. They appear in ***bold italic type*** throughout the book.

Meet the Packers

If football were a popularity contest, the Green Bay Packers would be in the **Super Bowl** every year. They have more fans in more places than any team in the **National Football League (NFL)**. That may seem a little odd since the Packers play in the smallest city in the league.

Green Bay, Wisconsin is a quiet town located on an arm of Lake Michigan. On game days, however, it explodes with excitement. The Packers have a glorious history and a great *tradition*. Every Sunday, they add a new chapter to one of the most incredible stories in sports. The fans, you see, own the team!

This book tells the story of the Packers. They are a year older than the NFL, and they still play football the old-fashioned way. When Green Bay's players take the field, they know exactly what is expected of them: Run fast, **block** well, tackle hard, and *never* forget who you are playing for.

Robert Ferguson and Mark Tauscher celebrate a scoring pass by Brett Favre. Favre holds almost every Green Bay passing record.

Way Back When

The most popular team in the NFL got its start with a case of tonsillitis. The patient's name was Curly Lambeau. He had been a high-school football star in Green Bay before heading to college to continue his career. In 1919, Lambeau returned home to recover from a throat infection. One day, he ran into a newspaperman named George Calhoun. They began talking about football and decided to start a team. Lambeau worked as a *shipping clerk* for Indian Packing. The company gave him $500 for uniforms and let his players practice in the empty lot next to the factory. Lambeau called the team the Indian Packers.

Rather than sell tickets to their games, the Packers passed a hat among their fans, who put money in it to be divided among the players. After two seasons playing nearby teams, the Packers joined the **American Professional Football Association**. In 1922, the league's name was changed to the National Football League. Over the next few years, Lambeau built a

LEFT: Johnny "Blood" McNally, Curly Lambeau, and Packers fan Paul Burke pose for a picture in 1932. **RIGHT**: The 1943 NFL Guide features Don Hutson, the league's top player the previous season.

strong team, which included Red Dunn, Johnny "Blood" McNally, Lavvie Dilweg, Mike Michalske, Verne Lewellen, Cal Hubbard, and Dick O'Donnell. They were crowned NFL champions each year from 1929 to 1931.

With Lambeau coaching the team, the Packers continued their great success. They played for the **NFL Championship** in 1936, 1938, 1939, and 1944. During that time, Green Bay was led by running back Clarke Hinkle, receiver Don Hutson, and quarterbacks Arnie Herber and Cecil Isbell.

The Packers fell on hard times during the 1950s. Their luck improved in 1959, when they hired Vince Lombardi to coach the team. Lombardi convinced his players that the key to winning was *executing* his plays exactly as they were diagrammed. For the next *decade*, the Packers were the best team in football. They won five NFL Championships and also the first two Super Bowls.

The heart of that team was its offensive line. It starred Jim Ringo, Jerry Kramer, Fuzzy Thurston, Forrest Gregg, and Bob Skoronski. They protected Green Bay's quarterback, Bart Starr, who was joined in the **backfield** by Paul Hornung and Jim Taylor. Green Bay's defense featured Ray Nitschke, Henry Jordan, Willie Davis, Herb Adderley, and Willie Wood.

The Packers had their ups and downs during the 1970s and 1980s. After Mike Holmgren became Green Bay's coach in 1992, however, the team went 13 years in a row without a losing season. Their leader on the field was Brett Favre, a fearless quarterback who played with great joy and *intensity*.

Joining Favre in the huddle were other top players, including Sterling Sharpe, Antonio Freeman, Robert Brooks, Dorsey Levens, and Ahman Green. The Packers defense starred Reggie White, LeRoy Butler, Gilbert Brown, Santana Dotson, and Darren Sharper. The Packers played in two Super Bowls during the 1990s and won one. It was the 12th championship in team history.

LEFT: Brett Favre, Green Bay's greatest quarterback ever.
ABOVE: Reggie White, whose nickname was "Minister of Defense."

The Team Today

The Packers are accustomed to success. They are the only NFL team that has won three championships in a row—and they have done that twice! Beginning in the 1990s, Green Bay fans had the pleasure of watching one of history's greatest quarterbacks, Brett Favre. He set a new *standard* of excellence that the team has tried to live up to ever since.

When Green Bay fans look on the field today, they see the beginning of an exciting new era. The names and faces of the Packers may change, but their goals will always be the same. Each season, the team hopes to finish at the top of the **National Football Conference (NFC)** and go to the Super Bowl.

The challenge for the Packers is to find new players who will keep their winning tradition alive. In recent seasons, they have added young stars such as A.J. Hawk, Aaron Kampman, Bubba Franks, and Donald Driver. They have also looked for talented **veterans** who can fill leadership roles. As the Packers have proven in the past, that is a plan that wins championships.

Donald Driver and Ruvell Martin perform a midair bump after a Green Bay touchdown.

Home Turf

The Packers play in Lambeau Field in Green Bay. The stadium opened on September 29, 1957. Vice President Richard Nixon was among the **celebrities** there for the event. Lambeau Field has been used by the Packers every year since. Only two other stadiums—Fenway Park in Boston and Wrigley Field in Chicago—have been in **continuous** use longer.

A few years ago, the Packers updated their stadium. They did so without changing its look. With the exception of two large video scoreboards, most of the changes took place underneath the stands. The stadium now includes the Packers Hall of Fame, Packers **Pro** Shop, and several restaurants. Outside the stadium, there are statues of Curly Lambeau and Vince Lombardi.

BY THE NUMBERS

- *There are 72,922 seats in the Packers' stadium.*
- *The enclosed Lambeau Field Atrium is 366,000 square feet.*
- *Each spring, 2,000 fans come to the stadium to watch the NFL draft.*
- *The cost of building the stadium in 1957 was $960,000. The cost of modernizing it in 2002 was $295 million.*

Green Bay fans begin to fill up Lambeau Field prior to a game.

Dressed for Success

During their early years, the Packers' team colors were blue and gold. Their coach, Curly Lambeau, had once played for the University of Notre Dame, which also used those colors. Fans liked those uniforms. In fact, some called the Packers the "Bay Blues."

Over the years, the team also wore green uniforms from time to time. Coach Vince Lombardi liked that color best. When he took over the team, he changed the official colors to green and gold. Green Bay's uniforms have changed little since then.

Bobby Dillon
HALFBACK   GREEN BAY PACKERS

The Packers had been wearing plain gold helmets for many years when Lombardi arrived. In 1961, his equipment manager added the famous football-shaped G *logo* to the team's helmets. Though the logo's shape has changed ever so slightly, it remains in use today.

Bobby Dillon, Green Bay's top defensive player during the 1950s, wears the team's old blue and gold colors.

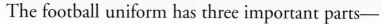

The football uniform has three important parts—

- Helmet
- Jersey
- Pants

Helmets used to be made out of leather, and they did not have facemasks—ouch! Today, helmets are made of super-strong plastic. The uniform top, or jersey, is made of thick fabric. It fits snugly around a player so that tacklers cannot grab it and pull him down. The pants come down just over the knees.

There is a lot more to a football uniform than what you see on the outside. Air can be pumped inside the helmet to give it a snug, padded fit. The jersey covers shoulder pads, and sometimes a rib protector called a flak jacket. The pants include pads that protect the hips, thighs, *tailbone*, and knees.

Football teams have two sets of uniforms—one dark and one light. This makes it easier to tell two teams apart on the field. Almost all teams wear their dark uniforms at home and their light ones on the road.

Mark Chmura, a star tight end from the 1990s, in the Packers' green and gold.

We Won!

The Packers were champions of the NFL three times before the league even held a championship game—in 1929, 1930, and 1931. In those days, the team with the best record was declared the champion. The Packers won thanks to the running and receiving of Johnny "Blood" McNally and a great defense led by Mike Michalske.

Green Bay's first title game came against the Boston Redskins in 1936. By this time, the team had the league's best passer in Arnie Herber, plus its top receiver, Don Hutson. Against Boston, Herber completed several long passes to Hutson and McNally, and the Packers won easily, 21–6.

Green Bay played the New York Giants for the NFL Championship in 1938 and 1939. The Giants won their first meeting, but Green Bay got revenge with a 27–0 shutout the following year. The two teams met for the title a third time in 1944, and the Packers won again, 14–7.

The Giants were also on the field when Green Bay won its next championship, in 1961. Quarterback Bart Starr threw three touchdown passes and Paul Hornung scored 19 points in a 37–0 victory. The defense—led by Ray Nitschke, Willie Wood, and Herb Adderley—caused five **turnovers**. One year later, the Packers beat the Giants again, 16–7.

The 1965 NFL Championship was played against the Cleveland Browns on a cold, wet field in Green Bay. The Packers controlled the game with their punishing rushing attack and simply wore down the Browns. Hornung and Jim Taylor combined for 201 yards on 45 carries in a mud-soaked contest that ended 23–12.

Green Bay beat the Dallas Cowboys for the NFL Championship in 1966 and 1967. Both games were very exciting, but they were no longer the season's final games. The NFL had agreed to join forces with its rival, the **American Football League (AFL)**. Part of the agreement called for an AFL-NFL championship, or Super Bowl. The Packers beat the Kansas City Chiefs 35–10 in Super Bowl I and the Oakland Raiders 33–14 in Super Bowl II. Starr was the **Most Valuable Player (MVP)** in both games.

LEFT: Green Bay champions Cal Hubbard, Johnny "Blood" McNally, Don Hutson, and Curly Lambeau reunite in 1963. **ABOVE**: Jim Taylor and Paul Hornung carry Vince Lombardi off the field after winning the 1965 NFL title.

The team's third Super Bowl victory—and its 12th NFL Championship—came 29 years later. Brett Favre led the Packers into battle against the New England Patriots in Super Bowl XXXI. In an exciting first half, Favre threw long touchdown passes to Andre Rison and Antonio Freeman. The Patriots battled back and scored a second-half touchdown to make the score 27–21.

Moments later, Desmond Howard returned New England's kickoff 99 yards for a touchdown. Favre threw a short pass to Mark Chmura for a **two-point conversion**, and Green Bay held on to win 35–21. Howard, who returned four kickoffs and six punts for a total of 244 yards, was voted Super Bowl MVP.

ABOVE: Donny Anderson heads for the end zone in Super Bowl II.
RIGHT: Antonio Freeman and Andre Rison, who each scored a touchdown in Super Bowl XXXI.

Go-To Guys

To be a true star in the NFL, you need more than fast feet and a big body. You have to be a "go-to guy"—someone the coach wants on the field at the end of a big game. Packers fans have had a lot to cheer about over the years, including these great stars …

THE PIONEERS

DON HUTSON   Receiver/Defensive Back

• Born: 1/31/1913   • Died: 6/26/1997   • Played for Team: 1935 to 1945

Don Hutson was the NFL's first great receiver. He was faster than the men who covered him and specialized in catching passes at full speed. Hutson was the first receiver to be regularly double-covered. He was also an excellent defensive player.

BART STARR   Quarterback

• Born: 1/9/1934   • Played for Team: 1956 to 1971

Bart Starr made winning look easy. He was a calm and confident leader who always seemed to have exactly the right call in the huddle. Starr led the NFL in passing three times and was the MVP of the first two Super Bowls.

PAUL HORNUNG — Running Back/Kicker

- BORN: 12/23/1935
- PLAYED FOR TEAM: 1957 TO 1962 & 1964 TO 1966

Paul Hornung was a point-scoring machine. He could run, pass, catch, and kick—and usually saved his best plays for the key moments in a game. In 1960, Hornung scored 176 points in 14 games.

JIM TAYLOR — Running Back

- BORN: 9/20/1935
- PLAYED FOR TEAM: 1958 TO 1966

Jim Taylor was the perfect fullback. He was a great blocker, a punishing runner, and an expert at turning short passes into long gains. Taylor was the man the Packers turned to late in games, when every yard and first down was crucial.

RAY NITSCHKE — Linebacker

- BORN: 12/29/1936 • DIED: 3/8/1998
- PLAYED FOR TEAM: 1958 TO 1972

Ray Nitschke was the man in the middle of Green Bay's great defenses of the 1960s. He was the team's hardest hitter and also one of its best athletes. Nitschke was the star of the 1962 NFL Championship game.

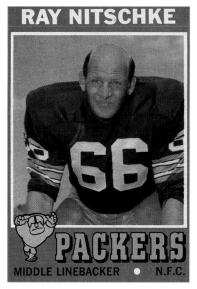

LEFT: Bart Starr   **TOP RIGHT**: Jim Taylor and Paul Hornung share a magazine cover in 1966.   **BOTTOM RIGHT**: Ray Nitschke

JAMES LOFTON Receiver

- BORN: 7/5/1956
- PLAYED FOR TEAM: 1978 TO 1986

James Lofton had sure hands and a track star's speed. No one in the NFL was harder to cover on deep passes. Lofton was voted to the **Pro Bowl** seven times in his nine seasons with the Packers.

STERLING SHARPE Receiver

- BORN: 4/6/1965
- PLAYED FOR TEAM: 1988 TO 1994

Any pass that Sterling Sharpe could touch, he usually caught. He was fast and tough and almost impossible to stop on short passes. Sharpe was at the top of his game when a neck injury forced him to retire.

REGGIE WHITE Defensive Lineman

- BORN: 12/19/1961   • DIED: 12/26/2004
- PLAYED FOR TEAM: 1993 TO 1998

When Reggie White joined the Packers in 1993, he turned them into a great defensive team. His ability to stop the run and rush the quarterback made all of his teammates better. White retired with the most sacks in NFL history.

BRETT FAVRE   Quarterback

• BORN: 10/10/1969   • FIRST SEASON WITH TEAM: 1992

Few quarterbacks have scared opposing defenses more than Brett Favre. From 1994 to 1998, he threw 176 touchdown passes and led the Packers to two Super Bowls. Favre was a great competitor who started more than 200 games in a row.

DONALD DRIVER   Receiver

• BORN: 2/2/1975   • FIRST SEASON WITH TEAM: 1999

Donald Driver went to his first training camp as an unknown seventh-round **draft pick**. He made so many amazing catches that the Packers had to keep him on the team. Driver became one of the best receivers in the NFL and was voted Green Bay's MVP in 2002 and 2005.

A.J. HAWK   Linebacker

• BORN: 1/6/1984

• FIRST SEASON WITH TEAM: 2006

Some players look like they were born to play football. From the moment A.J. Hawk stepped on the field for the Packers, he was right at home. With every game, he reminded Green Bay fans more and more of the team's great linebackers of the past.

On the Sidelines

It takes a big personality to coach a team in the NFL's tiniest town. Curly Lambeau, who guided the Packers for 29 years, could be loud and pushy. His players did not always like him, but they played very hard for him. Lambeau is remembered as one of the great *motivators* during the NFL's early days. From 1929 to 1944, his teams finished in first place eight times.

Football's most famous motivator may have been Vince Lombardi. He coached the Packers from 1959 to 1967. Lombardi demanded that his players be in great condition and that they run each play perfectly. Anything less, and he crashed into the locker room like a tornado. Under Lombardi, the Packers believed they could win every time they took the field—and their opponents did, too.

During the 1990s, Mike Holmgren coached the Packers. He could be strict, but he also could be a friend to his players. Holmgren had a master plan for the team's success, and it worked—the Packers finished first or second every year he coached them.

Mike Holmgren, the coach who guided the Packers to victory in Super Bowl XXXI.

One Great Day

Players and fans often call Lambeau Field the "frozen *tundra*." When the temperature plummets and the wind whips off Lake Michigan, the field—and the players—can get very cold very fast. The weather for the 1967 NFL Championship between the Packers and the Dallas Cowboys was worse than anyone could remember. The thermometer read 13 below zero at kickoff. The wind made it feel 30 degrees colder. No matter what the players did, they could not get warm.

Still, there was a game to be played. The Packers started quickly. Bart Starr threw two touchdown passes to Boyd Dowler in the first half. Dallas, however, recovered two Green Bay **fumbles** and scored twice to cut the Packers' lead to 14–10. Early in the fourth quarter, Dan Reeves of the Cowboys took a handoff and surprised the Packers when he stopped and threw a 50-yard touchdown pass.

The Packers trailed 17–14 with under five minutes left. They began the game's final **drive** on their own 32 yard line. Starr called a mixture of running plays and short passes, and moved the ball all the way to the 1 yard line with less than 60 seconds on the clock. He handed off to Donny Anderson twice, but the Cowboys stopped him both times.

With the seconds ticking down and no timeouts left, the Packers had a chance to tie the game with a **field goal**. Instead, Starr called a third run into the line. It was a gamble, because Green Bay had no way to stop the clock if the play failed. This time Starr carried the ball himself. He ran to the right and dove through a hole created by two of his **linemen**, Jerry Kramer and Ken Bowman. The Packers won 21–17. Forever after, this amazing game would be called the "Ice Bowl."

LEFT: The weather was brutally cold in the "Ice Bowl."   **ABOVE**: Boyd Dowler makes one of his two touchdown catches against the Cowboys.

Legend Has It

How did the "Lambeau Leap" start?

LEGEND HAS IT that LeRoy Butler first performed this celebration. In a 1993 game against the Los Angeles Raiders, the Packers needed a victory to make it to the playoffs. In the fourth quarter, after the Raiders completed a short pass, Butler forced a fumble with a hard tackle. Reggie White scooped up the ball and began running the other way, and then tossed it to Butler, who took it the rest of the way for a touchdown. Butler was so overjoyed that he jumped right into the stands, where the fans hugged and congratulated him. Today, the "Lambeau Leap" is a Green Bay tradition.

ABOVE: LeRoy Butler does the "Lambeau Leap."
RIGHT: Aaron Kampman is the leader of the pack at training camp.

Who are football's most famous bicycle riders?

LEGEND HAS IT that the Packers are. In the late 1950s, Vince Lombardi wanted the team to form a closer relationship with its young fans. He noticed that many fans rode their bikes to the team's training camp during the summer. Lombardi told the kids that his players would ride the bikes from the locker room to the practice field. It is a team tradition that continues to this day.

Who had the coolest name in the early days of the NFL?

LEGEND HAS IT that Johnny McNally did. During his seven seasons with the Packers—and 15 years as a player and coach in the NFL—he was known as Johnny Blood. While in college, McNally and a friend decided to play professional football. They did not want their school to find out, so they had to invent new names. On their way to tryouts, they passed a movie theater playing *Blood and Sand.* "That's it," McNally said. "I'll be Blood and you'll be Sand!"

It Really Happened

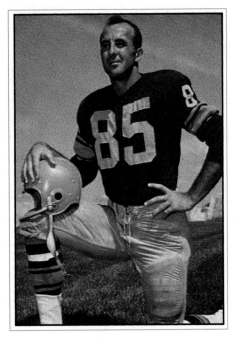

Vince Lombardi and his 35-year-old receiver Max McGee had what some people call a "love-hate" relationship. The super-strict coach loved McGee's ability to come off the bench and make big plays—and hated the sneaky ways McGee had of breaking his rules. The evening before the first Super Bowl, Lombardi warned his players that they had to be in bed by 11 P.M. McGee was in bed on time.

However, as soon as Lombardi went to sleep, McGee was on his way out of the hotel and into Los Angeles, where a night of Super Bowl parties awaited him. The receiver was not worried about the next day's game. Lombardi had no intention of using him, and McGee was planning on retiring after the game. He had played 11 seasons and just wanted to enjoy his last night as a Green Bay Packer. In the locker room the next day, a weary McGee reminded starting receiver Boyd Dowler not to get hurt. Old Max was in no shape to play.

Sure enough, Dowler injured his shoulder early in the game and had to spend the rest of the day on the bench. Lombardi barked out McGee's name, and the sleepy veteran jogged onto the field. Moments later, Bart Starr called his number. McGee cut across the middle and Starr threw a pass behind him. McGee reached back with his right arm and made a one-handed catch for a 37-yard touchdown.

McGee was now wide awake. He begged Starr to throw him the ball, and the quarterback did just that. McGee caught six more passes, scored another touchdown, and finished with 138 receiving yards. With his help, the Packers easily defeated the Kansas City Chiefs 35–10. McGee had so much fun that he decided to play one more season. A year later, he caught a 35-yard pass in Super Bowl II!

LEFT: Max McGee in his younger days with the Packers.
ABOVE: Vince Lombardi watches the action during Super Bowl I.

Team Spirit

The Packers are actually owned by their fans. In the 1920s, 1930s, and 1950s, the team needed help to stay in business. Each time, the fans of Green Bay came through and raised money for the club. Today, they are the last team in pro sports that is not owned by a company, family, or an individual. The Packers have more than 100,000 **stockholders**.

There are about 100,000 people living in the city of Green Bay. However, Packers fans are everywhere. The team has **season ticket** holders living in all 50 states, as well as in Canada, Japan, and Australia. Lambeau Field has been sold out since 1960, and there are now more than 70,000 people on the waiting list for tickets. Families at the top of that list have been on it for more than 20 years.

Wisconsin is famous for the cheese it produces, and many Green Bay fans wear yellow foam triangles on their heads during games. They call themselves "Cheeseheads."

There is no mistaking which team this Cheesehead is rooting for.

Timeline

In this timeline, each Super Bowl is listed under the year it was played. Remember that the Super Bowl is held early in the year and is actually part of the previous season. For example, Super Bowl XLI was played on February 4th, 2007, but it was the championship of the 2006 NFL season.

1929
Green Bay wins its first championship.

1949
Tony Canadeo becomes the first Packer to rush for 1,000 yards.

1919
The team is formed with help from a local meat-packing company.

1942
Don Hutson sets NFL receiving records with 74 catches and 17 touchdowns.

1967
The Packers win the first Super Bowl.

A souvenir pennant from the team's early days.

GREEN BAY PACKERS

BART STARR

PACKERS
QUARTERBACK • N.F.C.

Bart Starr, the MVP of Super Bowl I.

Desmond Howard, MVP of Super Bowl XXXI, enjoys a laugh after the game.

1983
John Jefferson is named co-MVP of the Pro Bowl.

1997
The Packers win Super Bowl XXXI.

2006
Brett Favre sets a record with his 15th 3,000-yard season in a row.

1980
James Lofton leads the NFC with 1,226 receiving yards.

1992
Sterling Sharpe leads NFL receivers in catches, yards, and touchdowns.

2003
Ahman Green leads the NFC with 1,883 rushing yards.

Sterling Sharpe

Ahman Green

Fun Facts

COMPLETE QUARTERBACK

In 2006, Brett Favre became the first player in history to complete 5,000 passes.

WING MEN

In 1940, the Packers became the first NFL team to travel to a game by airplane.

UNWANTED WILLIE

Despite being a star in college, Willie Wood was not drafted by a single pro team. He made the Packers as a **walk-on** in 1960 and played in the Pro Bowl eight times.

ROUGH START

In his first game as Packers coach in 1971, Dan Devine had to be carried off the field. A New York Giants' runner crashed into him on the sideline and broke his leg.

ALL THE TOOLS

The Packers found their first great quarterback, Arnie Herber, in their own clubhouse. The team had hired him as a handyman!

BACKING THE PACK

One of the Packers' most famous fans is Hollywood actor Matthew McConaughey. His father, Jim, was drafted by Green Bay in 1953 but did not make the team.

THUMBS UP FROM VINCE

Who was the greatest player on the championship Green Bay teams of the 1960s? Coach Vince Lombardi claimed that his right tackle, Forrest Gregg, was the "finest player" he had ever coached.

EYE ON THE PRIZE

Bobby Dillon was one of the NFL's best defensive backs in the 1950s. He **intercepted** 52 passes in eight seasons, despite being blind in one eye.

LEFT: Brett Favre   **ABOVE**: Forrest Gregg

Talking Football

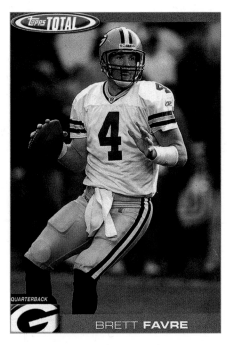

BRETT FAVRE
QUARTERBACK

"My dad never pushed me, but the big thing is that he helped me by going out in the backyard and playing with me."

—Bart Starr, on how his father helped him become a quarterback

"It's fun leading this offense!"

—Brett Favre, on why he played so many years

"There are a lot of places being built that seat a lot of people and have great food, but I don't think it's football unless it's being played at Lambeau Field."

—Sterling Sharpe, on the Packers' home stadium

"The **aura** around Lambeau and the people there—it's something that you just can't get out of your blood."

—Reggie White, on the Green Bay fans

ABOVE: Brett Favre   **RIGHT**: Green Bay lineman Jerry Kramer helps give Vince Lombardi a victory ride after Super Bowl II.

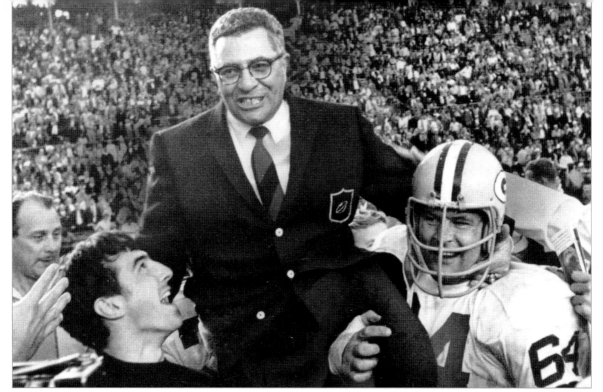

"Leaders are made, they are not born. They are made by hard effort, which is the price all of us must pay to achieve any goal that is worthwhile."

—*Vince Lombardi, on leadership*

"It was a wonderful thrill to have the team engulf me and pound me on the back and celebrate me like I was a running back."

—*Jerry Kramer, on his game-winning block in the 1967 NFL Championship*

"We couldn't stand Lombardi if we didn't win. That was always a motivation for us."

—*Willie Davis, on why the Packers tried extra hard to win for their extra strict coach*

For the Record

The great Packers teams and players have left their marks on the record books. These are the "best of the best" …

Jim Taylor

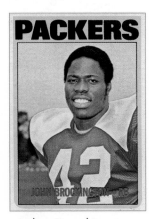

John Brockington

PACKERS AWARD WINNERS

WINNER	AWARD	YEAR
Don Hutson	NFL Most Valuable Player	1941
Don Hutson	NFL Most Valuable Player	1942
Vince Lombardi	NFL Coach of the Year	1959
Paul Hornung	NFL Most Valuable Player	1961
Jim Taylor	NFL Most Valuable Player	1962
Bart Starr	NFL Most Valuable Player	1966
Bart Starr	Super Bowl I MVP	1967
Bart Starr	Super Bowl II MVP	1968
John Brockington	NFL Offensive Rookie of the Year	1971
Fred Carr	Pro Bowl co-MVP	1971
Willie Buchanon	NFL Defensive Rookie of the Year	1972
John Jefferson	Pro Bowl co-MVP	1983
Lindy Infante	NFL Coach of the Year	1989
Brett Favre	NFL Most Valuable Player	1995
Brett Favre	NFL Offensive Player of the Year	1995
Brett Favre	NFL Most Valuable Player	1996
Desmond Howard	Super Bowl XXXI MVP	1997
Brett Favre	NFL co-Most Valuable Player	1997
Reggie White	NFL Defensive Player of the Year	1998

PACKERS ACHIEVEMENTS

ACHIEVEMENT	YEAR
NFL Champions	1929
NFL Champions	1930
NFL Champions	1931
Western Division Champions	1936
NFL Champions	1936
Western Division Champions	1938
Western Division Champions	1939
NFL Champions	1939
Western Division Champions	1944
NFL Champions	1944
Western Conference Champions	1960
Western Conference Champions	1961
NFL Champions	1961
Western Conference Champions	1962
NFL Champions	1962
Western Conference Champions	1965
NFL Champions	1965
Western Conference Champions	1966
NFL Champions	1966
Super Bowl I Champions	1966 *
Central Conference Champions	1967
NFL Champions	1967
Super Bowl II Champions	1967
NFC Central Champions	1972
NFC Central Champions	1995
NFC Central Champions	1996
NFC Champions	1996
Super Bowl XXXI Champions	1996
NFC Central Champions	1997
NFC Champions	1997
NFC North Champions	2002
NFC North Champions	2003
NFC North Champions	2004

** Super Bowls are played early the following year,
 but the game is counted as the championship of this season.*

Herb Adderley and Jim Ringo, stars of the 1962 championship team.

Pinpoints

The history of a football team is made up of many smaller stories. These stories take place all over the map—not just in the city a team calls "home." Match the pushpins on these maps to the Team Facts and you will begin to see the story of the Packers unfold!

TEAM FACTS

1   Green Bay, Wisconsin—*The Packers have played here since 1919.*

2   Toronto, Ohio—*Clarke Hinkle was born here.*

3   Louisville, Kentucky—*Paul Hornung was born here.*

4   Brooklyn, New York—*Vince Lombardi was born here.*

5   Washington, D.C.—*Willie Wood was born here.*

6   Jacksonville, Florida—*LeRoy Butler was born here.*

7   Montgomery, Alabama—*Bart Starr was born here.*

8   Gulfport, Mississippi—*Brett Favre was born here.*

9   Pine Bluff, Arkansas—*Don Hutson was born here.*

10   Birthright, Texas—*Forrest Gregg was born here.*

11   Fort Ord, California—*James Lofton was born here.*

12   Opole, Poland—*Chester Marcol was born here.*

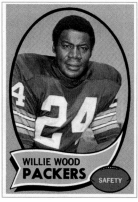

Willie Wood

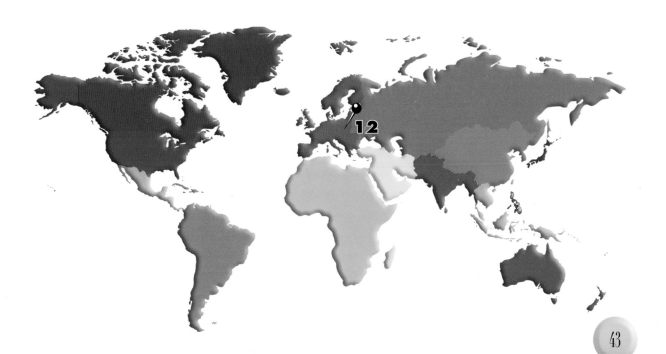

Play Ball

Football is a sport played by two teams on a field that is 100 yards long. The game is divided into four 15-minute quarters. Each team must have 11 players on the field at all times. The group that has the ball is called the offense. The group trying to keep the offense from moving the ball forward is called the defense.

A football game is made up of a series of "plays." Each play starts and ends with a referee's signal. A play begins when the center snaps the ball between his legs to the quarterback. The quarterback then gives the ball to a teammate, throws (or "passes") the ball to a teammate, or runs with the ball himself. The job of the defense is to tackle the player with the ball or stop the quarterback's pass. A play ends when the ball (or player holding the ball) is "down." The offense must move the ball forward at least 10 yards every four downs. If it fails to do so, the other team is given the ball. If the offense has not made 10 yards after three downs—and does not want to risk losing the ball—it can kick (or "punt") the ball to make the other team start from its own end of the field.

At each end of a football field is a goal line, which divides the field from the end zone. A team must run or pass the ball over the goal line to score a touchdown, which counts for six points. After scoring a touchdown, a team can try a short kick for one "extra point," or try again to run or pass across the goal line for two points. Teams can score three points from anywhere on the field by kicking the ball between the goal posts. This is called a field goal.

The defense can score two points if it tackles a player while he is in his own end zone. This is called a safety. The defense can also score points by taking the ball away from the offense and crossing the opposite goal line for a touchdown. The team with the most points after 60 minutes is the winner.

Football may seem like a very hard game to understand, but the more you play and watch football, the more "little things" you are likely to notice. The next time you are at a game, look for these plays:

PLAY LIST

BLITZ—A play where the defense sends extra tacklers after the quarterback. If the quarterback sees a blitz coming, he passes the ball quickly. If he does not, he can end up at the bottom of a very big pile!

DRAW—A play where the offense pretends it will pass the ball, and then gives it to a running back. If the offense can "draw" the defense to the quarterback and his receivers, the running back should have lots of room to run.

FLY PATTERN—A play where a team's fastest receiver is told to "fly" past the defensive backs for a long pass. Many long touchdowns are scored on this play.

SQUIB KICK—A play where the ball is kicked a short distance on purpose. A squib kick is used when the team kicking off does not want the other team's fastest player to catch the ball and run with it.

SWEEP—A play where the ball carrier follows a group of teammates moving sideways to "sweep" the defense out of the way. A good sweep gives the runner a chance to gain a lot of yards before he is tackled or forced out of bounds.

Glossary

AMERICAN FOOTBALL LEAGUE (AFL)—The football league that began play in 1960 and later merged with the NFL.

AMERICAN PROFESSIONAL FOOTBALL ASSOCIATION—The league that began in 1920 and became the National Football League in 1922.

BACKFIELD—The players who line up in back of the line of scrimmage. On offense, the quarterback and running backs are in the backfield.

BLOCK—Use the body to protect the ball carrier.

DRAFT PICK—A college player selected or "drafted" by an NFL team each spring.

DRIVE—A series of plays by the offense that "drives" the defense back toward its own goal line.

FIELD GOAL—A goal from the field, kicked over the crossbar and between the goal posts. A field goal is worth three points.

FUMBLES—Balls that are dropped by the player carrying them.

INTERCEPTED—Caught in the air by a defensive player.

LINEMEN—Players who begin each down crouched at the line of scrimmage.

MOST VALUABLE PLAYER (MVP)—The award given each year to the league's best player; also given to the best player in the Super Bowl and Pro Bowl.

NATIONAL FOOTBALL CONFERENCE (NFC)—One of two groups of teams that make up the National Football League. The winner of the NFC plays the winner of the American Football Conference (AFC) in the Super Bowl.

NATIONAL FOOTBALL LEAGUE (NFL)—The league that started in 1920 and is still operating today.

NFL CHAMPIONSHIP—The game played each year from 1933 to 1969 to decide the winner of the league.

PRO—A player or team that plays a sport for money. College players are not paid, so they are considered "amateurs."

PRO BOWL—The NFL's all-star game, played after the Super Bowl.

SEASON TICKET—A package of tickets for each home game.

SUPER BOWL—The championship of football, played between the winners of the NFC and AFC.

TURNOVERS—Fumbles or interceptions that give possession of the ball to the opposing team.

TWO-POINT CONVERSION—A play following a touchdown where the offense tries to cross the goal line with the ball from the 2 yard line, instead of kicking an extra point.

VETERANS—Players with great experience.

WALK-ON—A player who tries out for a team without being signed to a contract.

OTHER WORDS TO KNOW

AURA—An invisible quality that surrounds a person or place.

CELEBRITIES—People who are famous.

CONTINUOUS—Without pausing or stopping.

DECADE—A period of 10 years; also specific periods, such as the 1950s or 1960s.

EXECUTING—Carrying out a task as planned.

INTENSITY—The strength and energy of a thought or action.

LOGO—A symbol or design that represents a company or team.

MOTIVATORS—People who inspire others to action.

SHIPPING CLERK—A person who keeps track of goods sent from one place to another.

STANDARD—A guide or example.

STOCKHOLDERS—People who own shares of a business.

TAILBONE—The bone that protects the base of the spine.

TRADITION—A belief or custom that is handed down from generation to generation.

TUNDRA—A vast, treeless Arctic plain.

Places to Go

ON THE ROAD

GREEN BAY PACKERS
1265 Lombardi Avenue
Green Bay, Wisconsin 54304
(920) 569-7500

THE PRO FOOTBALL HALL OF FAME
2121 George Halas Drive NW
Canton, Ohio 44708
(330) 456-8207

ON THE WEB

THE NATIONAL FOOTBALL LEAGUE   www.nfl.com
  • *Learn more about the National Football League*

THE GREEN BAY PACKERS   www.packers.com
  • *Learn more about the Green Bay Packers*

THE PRO FOOTBALL HALL OF FAME   www.profootballhof.com
  • *Learn more about football's greatest players*

ON THE BOOKSHELF

To learn more about the sport of football, look for these books at your library or bookstore:

  • Fleder, Rob–Editor. *The Football Book*. New York, NY: Sports Illustrated Books, 2005.

  • Kennedy, Mike. *Football*. Danbury, CT: Franklin Watts, 2003.

  • Savage, Jeff. *Play by Play Football*. Minneapolis, MN: Lerner Sports, 2004.

Index

PAGE NUMBERS IN **BOLD** REFER TO ILLUSTRATIONS.

The Team

MARK STEWART has written more than 20 books on football, and over 100 sports books for kids. He grew up in New York City during the 1960s rooting for the Giants and Jets, and now takes his two daughters, Mariah and Rachel, to watch them play in their home state of New Jersey. Mark comes from a family of writers. His grandfather was Sunday Editor of *The New York Times* and his mother was Articles Editor of *The Ladies' Home Journal* and *McCall's*. Mark has profiled hundreds of athletes over the last 20 years. He has also written several books about New York and New Jersey. Mark is a graduate of Duke University, with a degree in History. He lives with his daughters and wife Sarah overlooking Sandy Hook, New Jersey.

JASON AIKENS is the Collections Curator at the Pro Football Hall of Fame. He is responsible for the preservation of the Pro Football Hall of Fame's collection of artifacts and memorabilia and obtaining new donations of memorabilia from current players and NFL teams. Jason has a Bachelor of Arts in History from Michigan State University and a Master's in History from Western Michigan University where he concentrated on sports history. Jason has been working for the Pro Football Hall of Fame since 1997; before that he was an intern at the College Football Hall of Fame. Jason's family has roots in California and has been following the St. Louis Rams since their days in Los Angeles, California. He lives with his wife Cynthia and recent addition to the team Angelina in Canton, Ohio.